iii

Nude With Pickle

A "Third World" Mystery

By Gus Hoo

Translated and With an Introduction
by James Hold

Nude With Pickle

Copyright © 2020 James Roy Hold

All rights reserved.

ISBN: 9798683517670

This is a work of fiction. Any resemblance to real people or actual events is coincidental. That said, the author requests the reader keep in mind the words of the Amazing Criswell in PLAN 9 FROM OUTER SPACE who challenged the viewer with: "Can you prove that it didn't happen?"

This is a work of fiction. Opinions expressed by characters herein should not be taken as those of the author.

Introduction

Gus Hoo was the pseudonym of a Guamian journalist whose work appeared exclusively in the now defunct *Guava Grapevine* in the native Chamorro language. There is much dispute as to Hoo's real identity and at this point no one can with any certainty say who Hoo was. The author was active from 1960 through 1990, after which he dropped from sight. A significant number of his stories remain untranslated.

The epic *Nude With Pickle* ran in biweekly installments of the *Guava Grapevine* for an incredible three years from January 1, 1965 through December 30, 1967. The text is woefully incomplete due to storm damage and general neglect. Even so, *Nude With Pickle* remains a worthwhile reading experience.

JH

Nude With Pickle

Nude With Pickle

Primo dicitur quod non significat aliquid.
— The Antiquities of Abonoteichus

An Invitation to Participate

Worlds within worlds... Coexisting on differing planes of reality... Very alike, yet all vastly different.

First World, Second World, Third... And how many more to follow? Inhabiting the same Time and Space... Separated only by rates of vibration...

Realms of existence where the same people occur; yet act in different ways, following different paths, making different choices than they do here.

Vibrations.

The ping of a tuning fork, the clang of an anvil, the thunder of a cloudburst; breaking down barriers, providing entry, offering brief glimpses into lands both similar and familiar, yet utterly unlike any we know. The way is there for us to access if we but open our eyes and follow our ears; the only boundaries are those of our imaginations and our willingness to explore.

Worlds which beckon us to enter... First World... Second World... Third...

Chapter 1

Those who walk in darkness stray ever from the light. This is true of man or woman, regardless of sex or gender. To travel a dark path is to follow one's footsteps down ebon trails of shadowy blackness which the luckless perambulator can only reverse by directing his steps elsewhere. Provided he can do so before the ultimate doom overtakes him.

But just as oblivion crouched at every doorstep, so too did Waldemar O'Reilly wait outside the steps of the Green Bay Museum of Modern Culture, waiting for its doors to open. Only in such a manner could he gain access to the treasures therein; treasures his lustful heart sought for his own.

It was a gray and miserable day, as are all days in Wisconsin, and the sun which so graciously shed its warmth on the rest of the world denied its shining rays to that of the Cheesehead State. Great solar turbines along Lakes Michigan and Superior labored unceasingly to provide the artificial sunlight necessary for America's Dreary Land's survival. Somewhere in the distant past, settlers from the New World violated a sacred pact with an Oneota medicine man, resulting in the Winnebago Uprising. Over time, the mounting accumulations of recreational vehicles blocked the sun, and it fell to the foreign settlers to find new ways to light the sky.

But all that was in the past. It meant nothing to the modern-day Waldemar O'Reilly. Waldemar O'Reilly lived in the moment, and the moment was now. Or rather it would be "now" once he got inside. And so he folded his thin polyester jacket close to his emaciated frame and waited. He had gone over this day many times in his mind, had rehearsed it to the last minute until it could be performed with split-second precision. He checked his wristwatch once more, only to find it had frozen in the icy blasts of Wisconsin's everyday climate. Still he was not discouraged. Once inside he could take a moment to thaw before carrying out his plans.

And what were those plans, one might ask. Nothing less than to rob the city of its most prized possession. In fact, the city's only thing of value. That being an autographed football bearing the signatures of that Holy Trinity of the Gridiron: Johnny Unitas, Bart Starr, and Vince Lombardi.

Now those who live in more temperate and prosperous areas of the nation might say, "What?" And they would be justified doing so. Only one must remember the time and place of which we speak. Wisconsin, a hell-bound ice-hole with nothing going for it save a semi-mediocre sports franchise that specialized in playing on icy fields and in blizzardly conditions. Which is not to say Green Bay Packers games were not the stuff of legend, for indeed they were. And what made them legendary was the fact so few had ever witnessed them in person, the stadium itself being nothing more than an open-air igloo and the air so cold that TV and radio waves could not travel more than a few feet beyond its boundaries before falling to the ground, frozen solid by the arctic winds that swirled about.

And so it was no wonder that an autographed football should become a rare and prized possession, the circumstances of the signing occurring on one of the few days in Green Bay history when temperatures were low enough to permit the ink to flow from the fountain pen.

All this was not news to Waldemar O'Reilly. He knew the city, nay the entire state, depended on the football for its very existence, renting it to outside exhibitions and other museums for periods of time—Wisconsin itself had no tourist industry, conditions being adverse to such things—and in this way drawing much-needed income to keep the state solvent.

What specifically he intended to do once he gained possession of the football he was not sure. To hold it up for ransom would be pointless as the state had no income without it.

Why, even the governor and members of congress had to take on secondary jobs as haberdashers and barbers to supplement their incomes. Perhaps he might seek a buyer outside the state, a collector of rarities who would pay handsomely for it. Ah, but those things could be worked out later. The important thing for now was to seize the football and make away with it.

Something that was now within his grasp as he heard the guard unlock the museum's front door to allow the public inside.

Chapter 2

It has been said that one man's trash is another man's treasure. It has also been said that a man without toes should avoid wearing thong sandals. But then, no one would dream of wearing sandals in this sort of weather so the second statement was rather moot.

Moot, boot, root, or a toot in the snoot, Waldemar O'Reilly didn't give a hoot. His only focus was on the loot as he wended his way past display cabinets of farm implements and milking machines to the special wing wherein rested the sacred autographed football. It lay there ungraded and on open display. The museum director assumed no one would dare molest the object, and besides, they hadn't the budget to hire a special guard to watch over it. Thus it was with childlike ease that Waldemar O'Reilly slipped the city's most prized possession under his jacket and sauntered casually back to the front exit. The sole sentry watching the door raised an eyebrow at the sight of the bulge at Waldemar O'Reilly's throat, but the clever criminal dismissed it with a smile and a simple explanation of, "Goiter," and the watchman let him pass.

It was not until three days later that the theft was discovered. The Green Bay Museum of Culture received few visitors, for obvious reasons which need not be gone into, and it was not until the cleaning lady showed up for her weekly rounds that anyone noticed the theft. Alarms were raised, and the police called in, but all concurred it was much too late to do anything about it.

"Gadzooks!" Mayor Adlartok tore his hair and lamented. "What dastardly villainy is this to render our great city helpless?"

"Great city?" His aide regarded him in a sideways manner. "Do you really want the press to quote you on that?"

"You're right," the mayor reconsidered. "Make that our fair city."

"Fair?" The aide pointed out the window. "Shouldn't we just leave it at 'city' and make the best of it?"

Inspector Tonraq of the Metropolitan Police was more patriotic however. "Of course it's a great city," he bellowed. "The very fact we've advanced from ice fishing to become one of the biggest cheese producers in the nation must count for something."

"I'm sorry, sir," the mayor's aide showed contrition. "You are of course correct. It is only because doctors claim too much cheese is bad for you that I chose to downplay the fact."

"Bah! Doctors," Tonraq spat the word. "What do they know? Maybe some sissy state like California or Arizona might have a problem with it, but here in Wisconsin men are men. Tough men at that. And any arteries that can stand our frozen weather don't need to worry about a little cheese blocking them."

"Gentlemen, please!" Mayor Adlartok stepped between them. "I'm sure we can all agree on the health benefits of extra cheese. But this gets us no closer to solving the matter at hand. Our city faces economic ruin unless we can solve this crime."

"It seems to me, sir," the mayor's aide observed, "that solving this crime falls entirely in the purview of the police department. That is, after all, what they are paid for, and for you and I," he here indicated himself and the mayor, "to fret over the matter is both pointless and unnecessary. We are doing our jobs on the civic front; it is now up to Inspector Tonraq to fulfill his obligations on the enforcement side of things."

"Oh it is, is it?" Tonraq reddened. "And just what do you suggest—?"

"It is not up to ms or the mayor to suggest anything," the aide fired back. "This is your area of expertise—supposedly, if your résumé is to be believed. Therefore I strongly suggest—"

Whatever it was the mayor's aide was about to suggest remained unsuggested as the man suddenly found himself lying on the floor with the burly form of Inspector Tonraq atop of him, his hands at his throat. It was all Mayor Adlartok could do to separate them.

"Gentlemen," he shouted. "If such either of you can be called. I'm ashamed at this public display of animosity. If this is your response to our current crisis then we may as well give up now and let the city crumble. Now what have you to say for yourselves?"

Chapter 3

For a long time neither man spoke. Feathers had been ruffled, perhaps under the stress of the moment, perhaps under the pressure of professional jealously. Rather than apologize, both sought neutral corners, there to sulk in silence as the disheartened mayor looked on.

"I was about to add," the aide said after a long silence, "that I checked with the city auditor and for us to offer a reward for the football's safe return is out of the question. We simply haven't the funds for it after fixing the potholes in the administration building parking lot."

The mayor sighed, but before he could say anything the aide went on.

"I did though contact the principals involved, that being the persons whose autographs appear on the ball, and both Johnny Unitas and Bart Starr have agreed to put up $1000 toward its recovery."

"That's something anyway," the mayor applauded. "Good work, Alphonse."

Alphonse, the aide, nodded humbly.

"What about Lombardi?" Inspector Tonraq demanded. "Doesn't he have an interest in this as well?"

"Coach Lombardi," Alphonse coughed, slightly embarrassed, "is a frugal man who—"

"He's a blasted tightwad," Tonraq, who happened to be a Vikings fan, threw in.

"It does seem odd," Mayor Adlartok agreed. "One would think it the least he could do after all the city has done to support him through his many losing seasons."

"Hmm," Tonraq tapped his chin in deep thought. "One might almost suspect he had an ulterior motive in refusing to help."

"Surely you don't think—" Adlartok didn't finish the sentence. He didn't need to. The same thought flashed across everyone's brain, the possibility that the coach might somehow be in on the deal. After all, when it came to football, no one could be said to be above suspicion.

"I think it merits looking into," Tonraq concluded, and the others concurred.

As a result, the evening newspapers, whose ears were everywhere, carried special editorials speculating as to the Green Bay coach's unwillingness to support his city, questioning his civic pride, demanding he live up to his civil duty, and calling on him to account for his egregious actions. Picket lines formed outside the coach's house and he was assailed with snowballs as he went to and from his mailbox which was stuffed with hate mail. Cries of "Give Us Back Our Balls," although technically inaccurate since only one ball was involved, became the order of the day. So bad did the situation escalate that the coach was unable to attend football practice and had to phone in his plays, all five of them, to the stadium where his assistants took charge of the games.

The results were telling. The one-time sports god whose effigies once sat alongside those of Mother Mary on household mantles now fueled bonfires as worshippers deserted him in droves. And drove great distances to desert him. Never what one would call a handsome man, the coach grew ever more haggard and disheveled in appearance and even his own dog deserted him.

Now a god can endure many things, poor attendance, empty collection plates, lousy singing by the choir, but the one thing they cannot withstand is the loss of followers. And it was just at the point where the infamous tightwad was reluctantly on the verge of opening his pocketbook that Police Detective Björn Yisterdae burst into Inspector Tonraq's office, nearly tearing the door off its hinges as he breathlessly announced, "Sir! We've caught a break!"

[The next two installments, January 9 and 15, 1965, suffer water damage and are mostly illegible. They appear to be a discourse on the great solar turbines along Lakes Michigan and Superior that provided the artificial sunlight necessary for Wisconsin's survival, along with a lengthy lamentation for the day when they cease to operate. We skip ahead to January 16, 1965 and Chapter 6.]

Chapter 6

Meanwhile, despite the impending doom that threatened the state, Inspector Tonraq stared at Detective Yisterdae and repeated, "You say you caught a break? Hot diggety!"

He did not need to ask to what case the detective referred. There was but one case occupying the minds of all Cheeseheads at the moment.

"Well, not exactly," Björn Yisterdae backed off from his earlier statement. "The last time I caught a brake I got grease all over my uniform and it took a dozen bleachings to get it cleaned."

"I always wondered why you wore white when the rest of the department sported blue. Anyway, go on."

"It's like this, sir. There was a girl in the museum at the time of the theft, an art student by the name of Yumiko Raskolnikov, working on a reproduction of the famous Dagwood Hymnau painting *Nude With Pickle*. She was sitting off in a corner at the time and—"

"Wait a minute," Tonraq interrupted. "Nude With What?"

"*Nude With Pickle*," Yisterdae repeated. "It took second place at last year's Cannes Film Festival."

"A painting won an award at a film festival?" Tonraq was understandably confused.

Yisterdae nodded. "The artist, Hymnau, had a camera crew follow him around as he completed the work."

"Hmm," the Inspector inclined his head in thought. "Then if I hired a film team follow me around on this case..."

"Sir?"

"Yes?"

"About the witness."

"Oh, right. Go on."

"Well, sir, Miss Raskolnikov, who I'm told is quite talented, upon seeing the robbery in progress, quickly painted the thief's head in place of the one in the original painting, giving us a perfect description of the culprit. Now all we need do is to send photographs of her painting to the news outlets and hope for a speedy arrest."

"Not so fast, Detective. I'd like to interview this Raskolnikov woman myself first, if you don't mind."

"Jeepers, Inspector; I didn't mean to overstep."

"Nevermind. Have my car brought around and I'll be down shortly."

Tonraq waited for the detective to leave, then picked up his phone. "Hello? AAA Media Services? You're an independent outfit, correct? Work for hire? Good. I'd like to have a camera crew accompany me to..."

* * *

Yumiko Raskolnikov, it turned out, was a sort of beatnik-hippie chick in leotards and a sweater. When Tonraq and his film team arrived at the museum she was sitting in a corner before the famous *Nude With Pickle* painting, perched behind a big easel while precociously singing a David Bowie song that had yet to be written: "*The Sun Machine is coming down, and we're gonna have a party.*"

"The girl's some sort of subversive," was Tonraq's first thought as he sized her up. He waited for the camera man's signal then asked his first question. "You're Yumiko Raskolnikov?"

"Si," she comprendido'd.

"Can you speak up a little," the soundman called out. "I didn't get that."

"Si," the girl repeated. "Soy Raskolnikov."

"Great. And is it true you saw the man who stole the football?"

"Si. Vi al ladrón." And she turned her easel to face the camera.

"Wonderful," Inspector Tonraq rubbed his hands with glee. "I should have the case solved in no time. Are you boys getting all this?"

Chapter 7

Sadly for Inspector Tonraq, "no time" proved a literal truth because at no time did he come any closer to finding the thief than on the day he started. The springtime blizzards continued to blow, leaving ten-foot drifts everywhere; the great solar turbines continued to function sporadically; and the film cameras continued to record the lack of progress daily.

"Dagnabbit!" Tonraq pounded his desk while Mayor Adlartok paced the room, helplessly attempting to avoid the camera and microphone cords that were spread out across the floor of the inspector's office. "There's no way the bounder can elude our manhunt without outside help. He must have an accomplice somewhere."

"You don't suppose—"

There was a loud crash as the mayor tripped over a wire.

"Merciful Heavens," Tonraq rushed forward. "Is everything all right?"

"I believe so," Mayor Adlartok began. "I don't think I broke anything."

"Not you," Tonraq snarled. "I was asking if the camera was still working."

"That's another thing I wanted to bring up, Tonraq. Just how much is this costing us?"

"Trust me, sir," Tonraq put an arm around the mayor's shoulder, "when this wins first prize at Cannes for Best Documentary... Picture it now: our names on the screen—"

"Whose name comes first?"

"Well, naturally, me being the one to solve the case..."

"Which you have yet to do, I might add. It's been three weeks since you sent those photos to the newspapers and you have yet to turn up a single lead."

"That's the whole point I was starting to make when you interrupted me. You boys are getting this, right? Mayor, it's time we stopped pussyfooting around and got tough with these jokers. And Joker Number One on my list is Lombardi. His actions since the day of the theft have done nothing to remove him from suspicion. I say we drag him down to the station and have the boys go over him with a rubber hose."

"Tonraq?"

"Give him a good working over until he spills everything he knows."

"Tonraq!"

"What!"

"Are you sure this is the sort of thing you want on film?"

"Oh... Right. You boys can edit that part out, can't you?"

The film crew nodded affirmative.

"Good. Then let's get a warrant and—"

"Tonraq."

"What? For heaven's sake, why do you keep interrupting me?"

"Because, Inspector, if you spent half as much time reading the news as you do trying to make it, you'd know that Coach Lombardi lit out for Washington, DC the same day you released those pictures to the papers. Something about a future coaching job once his days here are done."

"Great Cesar's ghost, why doesn't anybody tell me these things? Quick, have the DA file extradition papers to get him back. Call our congressman and have him—"

"Yes?"

"You say he lit out? How?"

"Caught an LC-130 out of Ontario."

"Ontario? How'd he get—"

"He skated. Superior was frozen."

Tonraq hung his head with extreme disappointment.

"They always said the man could walk on water. I guess here he went and proved it."

[The next 8 installments, January 23 to February 19, 1965, are encrusted with salt brine and impossible to read, forcing us to move on to February 20, Chapter 16, and the introduction of the story's chief protagonist.]

Chapter 16

The man who walks in darkness is blinded by the night. The man who walks in sunshine is blinded by the light. The only "he" who truly sees must keep to the twilight, and even then his vision is suspect.

Tercero Mundo, famed PPI, or Paranormal Private Investigator, was tall and exceedingly gaunt. He had inherited a heavy mantle from his father, which is why he wore an Inverness coat instead. He did however hang onto his father's slouch hat, believing it lent an air of mystery to his appearance. Despite his great height, sitting or standing, Tercero Mundo's feet always remained two inches above the ground.

Bob "Gucci-Only" Flint published a successful line of magazines featuring girls on the cover and no cover on the girls. He had a penthouse office atop the largest building in Milwaukee, which in any state other than Wisconsin would place it on the third floor. He had earned his nickname by virtue of the fact he adamantly refused to endorse any other brand of loafers. It was into these offices that Tercero Mundo directed his footsteps, treading lightly above the plush carpet that had cushioned the feet of so many beautiful women in its day.

Wasting no time with needless formalities, Tercero Mundo walked straight to the receptionist's desk where a topless woman greeted him.

"Yes?" she smiled sweetly. "May I help you?"

"You may," he answered in a deep, throaty voice. "I'm here to see Mr Flint."

"One moment please." She got on the intercom. "Mr Flint? There's a man here to see you."

"Who is it?" asked the accented voice from the other side.

"I'm not sure," the woman gave Tercero Mundo the once-over. "It's either John Carradine or the Shadow."

"Show him in."

"Yes, sir." The woman rose from her desk, revealing she was not only topless but bottomless as well, and conducted Tercero Mundo into the inner sanctum of Bob "Gucci-Only" Flint's private office.

"Welcome, Mr World," Gucci-Only greeted him warmly. "Please, have a seat."

"Thank you," the paranormal investigator responded. "And please, call me Third."

"Oh?" Gucci-Only looked around. "Are there two more ahead of you?"

"No, sir. I meant that is my first name."

"Your first name is third? Is this some Abbot and Costello routine?"

"Perhaps we should buzz your secretary," Tercero Mundo suggested.

"Well," Gucci-Only hesitated, "I generally don't go in for threesomes; especially with another guy."

"I meant to check your appointment calendar."

"Ah, right." Gucci-Only pressed a button and a naked girl, a different one than the receptionist, came in.

"Bambi, what's on my schedule for today?"

"Coffee stains mostly, but let me check." She put on a pair of thick glasses. "You have Primo Carnera, the Italian boxer followed by Segundo Cernadas, an Argentine actor..."

"Primero is second?"

"Technically Primero is first."

"Then who's second?"

"No, Gus Hoo's your four o'clock."

"I don't want go guess who's my four o'clock."

"Gus Hoo's a short story writer out of Guam."

"Look, Bambi, I'm not interested in guessing. All I'm asking is who's second?"

"Well, sir, strictly speaking, Segundo is second, only we have him third."

"I thought this guy was third. Why am I seeing him now?"

"You don't see Hymnau until tomorrow."

"I don't see him...now...tomorrow?" Gucci-Only blinked in confusion.

"Dagwood Hymnau, the artist who painted *Nude With Pickle*."

"Why would a man paint with pickles? Why not oils or acrylics?"

"Perhaps if I came back mañana," Tercero Mundo rose to leave."

"Can he do that?" Gucci-Only asked Bambi.

"Only if he wants to get in trouble for impersonating a Spanish diplomat. Max Mañana is from the embassy in Barcelona."

"So that means I have to see him now?"

"You don't see Hymnau until tomorrow."

"Here we go again." Gucci-Only threw his hands in the air. "This is certainly screwed up."

"No," Bambi smiled patiently as she pointed to Tercero Mundo, "he isn't. Sir Tinley Scrudup isn't scheduled to come in until next week."

Here Bob "Gucci-Only" Flint opened his jaw as if to speak and pointed a finger at nothing; after which he froze. He remained that way for ten minutes until finally Tercero Mundo asked, "Does he do this often? Go catatonic I mean."

"It's the pressure of operating a popular magazine. The tension gets to him and..." She stepped around the desk to glance down at his lap, "Yep, he's tense all right," and started to get down on her knees. "Generally when this happens I—"

"Suppose I give you a few minutes," Tercero Mundo once again rose from his chair.

"Better make it an hour," Bambi recommended. "Meanwhile you can wait in the lounge. We have a lot of girls there who can entertain you while you wait."

Chapter 17

An hour later, Gucci-Only was back to normal, his tension having been alleviated, with a huge smile on his face. Tercero Mundo also wore a huge smile, not that he'd had any tension that needed alleviating, but the girls in the lounge had been exceedingly nice to him all the same.

"Now suppose we get down to business," Gucci-Only proposed. "Your reputation precedes you..."

Tercero Mundo glanced down and saw his fly was still open. He quickly corrected this.

"As I was saying," Gucci-Only pretended not to notice, "I've heard of you and the many amazing things you've accomplished..."

"Did those girls talk?"

"Knock it off and listen, would you? Like everyone else, I know about the theft of Green Bay's sacred football. I've no interest in that. I've always been a Vikings fan myself. What I am interested in is the reproduced painting of *Nude With Pickle* by that Raskolnikov girl."

"You want her for your next centerfold?"

"That bony thing? Don't make me laugh. My interest is in the face she painted of the man who committed the theft. I could not help but notice he had...well, a rather large appendage."

"I think that was the pickle."

"Maybe, maybe not. It's the image that counts. What I want you to do is to track that man down and bring him here to me."

"You're going to turn him in for the $2000 reward?"

Gucci-Only took a moment to stare at Tercero Mundo and the PPI feared he might have to call Bambi in again to bring him out of another catatonic trance. Fortunately this only went on for a minute and the magazine publisher continued.

"$2000 is peanuts compared to what I have in mind. Look at it this way, Mundo. The adult video market is a rapidly expanding industry."

"Parts of it are growing anyway."

"Magazines won't last forever. The future is in films. And I want in on the ground floor."

"From what I understand, Mr Flint, the floors of those places can be quite sticky."

"I'm talking home videos, Mundo; featuring the man with the most enormous...thingy...in the business."

"You're sure it's that...enormous?"

"We'll film it to look that way. Look, the reproduction of that foto in all the newspapers has given us the sort of advanced publicity a man can only dream of. It's a once in a lifetime deal to cash in. And don't think I'm the only guy to think of it. That rabbit guy in California has the same idea, not to mention all those British tabloids."

"British tabloids?"

"I told you not to mention them. The problem is he's too well hidden and no one knows where he is. Unless you find him."

Tercero Mundo understood. Paranormal Private Investigators are not beyond the need for money.

"And what do I get in return?"

"Fifteen percent of the profits from each picture."

"Fifteen?"

"All right; make it twenty."

"Sold."

A handshake followed, Gucci-Only being a man of his word, and Tercero Mundo set off on his quest to find the man with the enormous pickle.

[We encounter still another instance of damaged text, presumably dealing with Tercero Mundo's search for Waldemar O'Reilly, forcing us to jump to March 26, 1965 and middle of Chapter 25.]

Chapter 25
(joined in progress)

Benjamin Blayney Barthelme held up his hands, shielding his eyes from the penetrating glare of Tercero Mundo's awesome gaze.

"Honestly, Mundo, I swear I don't know a thing. Since our last encounter I've gone straight. I can prove it. Take a look at this."

He produced a sheaf of papers.

"While I was in prison I took a course in Evelyn Wood Speed Reading Dynamics. I learned a lot, quick. At the same time I saw all these Evangelists dropping by every weekend doing missionary work, trying to convert the thugs and mugs to Christianity. A lot of the cons gave it a try, but they backed out because the Bibles they were issued were too bulky and the language too archaic for them to wade through. That's where I saw an opportunity to save men's souls and make a few bucks on the side."

"How's that?" Tercero Mundo lightened his gaze.

"Like this," Triple-B hurried on. "I decided to use my speed reading abilities, along with the memory skills it taught me, to compile a minimalist condensation of the essential points of Old and New Testament belief into an easy to read 10-page tract. I'm calling it *The Bible, A Condensed Version for Today's Busy Reader*. I have a publisher lined up and everything. So why, I ask, would I want to get involved in the theft of a stupid football? Beside which, I happen to be a Twins fan."

"Let me see those papers," Tercero Mundo held out a bony hand into which Triple-B placed them.

Glancing over the manuscript, the Paranormal PI examined the document. True to his word, the former crook had indeed produced a remarkably clear and concise condensation of many of the key points relating to both Old and New Testament texts. Among them were:

In first book of the Bible Adam and Eve were created from an apple.

*The passengers on the Ark could not play cards because Noah sat on the deck.

* Lot's wife was a pillar of salt by day and a ball of fire by night.

* Moses wandered 40 years in the desert. When he finally settled down, he picked the only piece of land without a drop of oil under it.

* The 10 Commandments were carved in stone, which made them difficult to read in bed at night. The seventh one states, "Thou shalt not admit adultery".

*Joshua led the Hebrews in the battle of Geritol while Samson slew the Philistines with the axe of the apostles.

* Solomon had 100 wives and 700 porcupines. As a result, the Jews had trouble throughout their history with unsympathetic Genitals.

* Jesus' birth came about because Mary had an immaculate contraption.

* Jesus had 12 opossums, one of whom was Matthew; among the others were John, Paul, George, and Ringo.

* When Nathanael asked, "Can any good thing come from Nazareth?" Philip played "Hair

of the Dog," resulting in the first ever shout out for "More cowbell!"

** Salome danced in 7 veils in front of King Harrod's. For this she received John the Baptist's head on a platter, which she later exchanged for a tea service.*

** Paul preached acrimony, which is another name for marriage. Additionally, a Christian should have only one wife. This is called monotony.*

** When the Four Hoarse Men of the Apocalypse come riding up, you can hang onto your house, your spouse, and your chickens; but be prepared to kiss your ass goodbye.*

Tercero Mundo returned the manuscript, greatly impressed at Triple-B's efforts.

"Like I said," Triple-B rushed on, "I have a publisher lined up. They'll be available in Buc-ee's stores all across Texas, located next to their 86-ounce insulated drink mugs. There's even a sign saying you'll finish reading the book long before you get done drinking the soda."

Tercero Mundo smiled, happy to see another man had turned his back on a life of crime. He wished Benjamin Blayney Barthelme good luck and resumed his search for the man with the pickle.

Chapter 26

Jackson Shirley was not a crook. He'd never been a crook, and he had no reason to consider becoming one. He was however one of the few friends in whom Tercero Mundo felt comfortable confiding.

The frustrations of his fruitless search were taking their toll on him and he needed a place to go where he could relax for a while and let his mind rest. In times such as these, Jackson Shirley always provided a needed distraction.

Jackson Shirley was a writer. His debut novel, *We Have Always Haunted the Hill Castle*, had earned him a fortune to where he need never write another. But unlike that Alabama bird woman, Jackson lived by the motto that writers write. And this he continued to do.

"Mundo!" Jackson met his guest enthusiastically at the door. "Come in! Come in! Take a load off. What brings you here? No, wait, before you tell me, let me read you my latest short story. I'm including it in my upcoming tennis anthology, *Man, Go Watch a Set*."

Tercero Mundo listened with interest to the disturbing tale, titled "The Giraffle," set in a small New England village where the residents, having grown weary of lobbing stones at people, chose instead to stage animal stampedes. Something goes wrong however. Kids at play inadvertently blast a car horn, causing the already nervous creatures to bolt ahead of schedule. Several prominent citizens are killed. The giraffe goes on the lam—which doesn't do the lamb any good—but is finally caught. At his trial, the giraffe pleads not guilty due to diminished faculties. "I was high at the time." The pig argues it was in his nature. "I ham what I ham." The chickens show amazing indifference, not giving a cluck. Eventually all are found guilty and sentenced to be barbecued.

"So, what do you think?" asked Jackson once he'd finished.

Tercero Mundo hesitated before answering.

"You know, for an accomplished writer, you certainly use a lot of adverbs."

"Don't tell me you're part of that movement that says to omit them," Jackson took umbrage. "Adverbs are a useful tool for telling when, where, why, or under what conditions something happened. Anyone who says not to use them is an idiot."

"I was only saying..." Tercero Mundo trailed off weakly.

"They were good enough for Lovecraft, Howard, and Bloch." Jackson went on vehemently, "and they're good enough for me!"

"Perhaps I picked a bad time," Tercero Mundo got up to leave. "I should go get drunk instead."

"I suppose next you'll want to criticize my use of exclamation points!"

Tercero Mundo reached the door, heaving a heavy sigh as he pinched the bridge of his nose.

"I make frequent references to the weather as well!"

Tercero Mundo closed the door behind him. Jackson yanked it open and called after him.

"And I use modifiers other than 'said'!"

Tercero Mundo was halfway down the sidewalk when Jackson called out for the last time.

"If you squeeze all the juice from a lemon you're left with nothing but a useless husk!"

A final thundering slam appeared to indicate he was done.

Tercero Mundo hurried on.

"Lemons?" he told himself. "Perhaps a shot of tequila would be just what the doctor ordered."

Chapter 27

One hour later, Tercero Mundo was sitting alone at his table, a bottle of tequila at his right and a salt shaker and bowl of lemons at his left, when an irate Jackson Shirley stormed into the bar and slammed a single page of typewritten script before him.

"I suppose this is more to your liking," he bellowed.

Tercero Mundo glanced down, uninterested.

"I didn't bother with a title," Jackson raged on. "Minimalist work doesn't need them."

Seeing he had no choice in the matter, Tercero Mundo picked up the single page and read:

"Oh, John," said Sally. "I love the view from Lover's Lane."

"So do I," John said. "Now kiss me."

Although it was not sudden the car door was all the same ripped from its hinges and a brute dragged Sally from her seat.

"Oh, John," said Sally.

"Don't fear," John said. "I'll save you."

But the brute killed him and ran away.

*

"Bwahaha," the scientist said. "The storm I was not allowed to mention at the start of the story is brewing."

His assistant brought Sally inside.

"Master," he said. "I found a girl."

"Is she pretty?" the scientist said.

"I don't know," the assistant said. "We're not permitted to use physical descriptions. Does that mean I'm not a hunchback?"

*

The door opened and a policeman entered.

"Let go of the girl," he said.

"How did you find me?" the scientist said.

"I'd tell you," the policeman said, "but readers skip over those parts."

*

"Stop," said the scientist, coming close to using an exclamation point. "One more step and I throw this switch."

"Take that you," the policeman said and shot him.

" 'You' what?" said the scientist.

"I don't know," the policeman said.

"We're not allowed adjectives or adverbs either."

*

"Oh," said Sally. "My hero," she said.

"Now all is good," said she.

"Yes," the policeman said and took her in his arms.

"Yes," said God and saw that it was good.

"Yes," said Elmore Leonard and gave it seven on a ten scale.

"Who's Elmore Leonard?" Tercero Mundo asked once he'd finished reading.

Jackson stared, but said nothing, other than, "Well?"

"To tell the truth..." Tercero Mundo began, but before he could finish the sentence Jackson Shirley fled screaming into the night. It was a stormy one, by the way.

Tercero Mundo poured another drink, sliced another lemon, and went on as he had been doing; knowing Jackson Shirley would never open his door to him again.

[Here follows the most frustrating section of Nude With Pickle *in which 275 installments of the serial were rendered unreadable. In May 1976, Typhoon Pamela struck Guam causing millions of dollars of damage. As a result of its destruction, the* Guava Grapevine's *microfiche library was flooded and several years' worth of content were washed out to sea. Back issues from April 3, 1965 through November 28, 1967 were irredeemably lost. Scattered bits and pieces gleaned from tantalizing fragments reveal the story taking a darker turn. Said remnants are reproduced here, for what they may be worth.]*

"Very well, Mundo," the Baron rubbed the scar that ran down the side of his forehead. "I will answer your questions—provided you face three challenges. You need complete but two, although to fail even one is to die."

"Suppose I was to lose the second? How then would I accomplish the third?"

"I never said it would be easy. But if it's any comfort I won't charge you for the..."

*

"...twenty-five she-goats that were kept..."

*

"...hidden in the bishop's quarters."

*

An early morning chill lay over the land as the Ranger prepared to get underway. To his dismay, Tonto lay motionless in a profound state of slumber. The masked man prodded him with a booted toe but there was no response.

"Trouble getting started, stranger?" one of the townspeople asked.

"Yep," the Ranger nodded laconically. "My Injun won't turn over. I guess I'll have no choice but to..."

*

"...arrest you, Thérèse Raquin, for the murder of your husband, Camille Raquin."

"Let's not rush to judgement, Cochran," Mr Mason stepped in. "It's true you found Mrs

Raquin alone in the room with the victim, the stolen jewels in her purse and the murder weapon in her hand. Not to mention a vial of poison, a fireplace poker, a length of rope, and several kitchen knives at her side. And it's true she was heard threatening to kill Mr Raquin minutes before the murder took place. Still I'm convinced if you strip away all the glitz and glamour, you'll find that underneath that fancy designer dress is..."

*

...a festering swampland, a living tide of slime, seething through fen channels dripping with dead moss, and foul bubbles rising from the depths.

*

In his haste to flee the burning building, Tercero Mundo stumbled over what might have been an Egyptian gorilla, only it wasn't because such things don't exist. Instead he found it to be...

*

...a fifty-dollar gold piece stamped with the impression of William McKinley, riding...

*

...a blazing comet through...

*

...the women's dormitory. The doctor was taken aback to recognize...

*

...his own sister among the screaming throng, foaming at the mouth while demanding...

*

...a chocolate sundae with whipped cream and crushed walnuts. The soda jerk served it with haste and...

*

Following the customary practice of the time...

*

...she wrapped her sensuous lips around his...

*

...immense celery stalk. It was salty to the taste and she asked, "Are you sure you washed this thing?"

"It was purified only last week in the waters of Lake Minnetonka," he assured her. "I was forced to after I found it..."

*

...lying in a spreading pool of dark blood. The crooked lawyer was dead by his own hand; a ripe green banana where the pistol should have been. The coroner attributed the cause of death to...

*

...centuries-old demons, all extremely dangerous and horrifying, defying any clear description, other than to say...

*

...the veins stood out like shoestrings on a head of cabbage. The fact he had green hair only added to the effect.

[We can only lament the incalculable loss of narrative as the hero, Tercero Mundo, tracks the villain Waldemar O'Reilly by means unknown and methods unknowable. However until Time sees fit to bestow on us a better edition of the text we have no choice but to skip ahead to December 1, 1967 and Chapter 303.]

Chapter 303

"Psst!"

Yumiko Raskolnikov cocked her head to one side, thinking she'd heard a sound come from the potted plant behind her. She was at the Green Bay Museum of Modern Culture working on another reproduction of *Nude With Pickle*— her first attempt still in possession of Inspector Tonraq—while humming still another yet to be recorded David Bowie song, "*I...I wish I could swim...*" and she could not be sure if she'd heard anything or not.

"You!" The voice came again. "With the easel."

This time Yumiko did hear it. "Si?" she replied, turning to see the homely face of Coach Lombardi peering at her through the leaves of an artificial Dracaena.

"¡Dios mío!" Yumiko Raskolnikov leaped from her stool. "¡Un mono ha escapado del zoológico!"

"Oh, can it, sister," Lombardi growled. "Green Bay doesn't have a zoo. If it did do you think I'd waste my time drafting college linemen?"

"Ach, du bist Herr Trainer Lombardi!"

"Yes, and could you please stick to one language at a time; like say English perhaps?"

"Oui je sais—how you say?—parler anglais."

Lombardi sighed, figuring this was as good as it was going to get.

"Look, kid, just listen, okay? I'm in a lot of hot water because everyone thinks I had something to do with that football robbery."

"You found hot water? Here? In Green Bay?"

"Yes, and if you're good I'll let you have a pint. By the way, is that glass? I thought artists painted on canvas."

"I prefer mirrored surfaces. It reflects my mood."

"Yeah, I guess it would." Lombardi didn't know if that had been meant as a joke or not. The girl had too serious an expression to imagine her cracking a smile. "Here's the deal. I need your help in tracking down the thief. Everyone thinks I'm in on it but I'm not. That doesn't mean I don't have an idea who might be behind it. My problem is I don't have the freedom of movement to confront him openly. If the cops see me they'll haul me down to the station and work me over with a rubber hose. So I need to do it on the QT."

"And I am to be zis QT as you call it, nicht wahr?"

"It's almost closing time and it'll be dark soon. Pretend I'm your assistant. I'll carry your paints and your easel so it hides my face. Once we're safely outside and in your van I'll instruct you where to go. Get me there and I'll confront the guy I believe is behind the whole deal."

"And you want I do all this for a pint of hot water?"

"Make it two then."

"No! I do notheen for less zan zee entire gallon."

"Oy vey! Fine. It'll mean going without bathing for a week but I'll do it.

"Then it is set. You carry my paints...and my brushes...and my easel...and my stool...and my lunch box...and my—"

"What about the painting?"

"That nobody touches but me. I carry it myself, always."

"Hmm, you're pretty strong for such a bony thing. Have you ever thought of playing linebacker?"

Chapter 304

At the same time the conversation between Coach Lombardi and Yumiko Raskolnikov was taking place, Tercero Mundo was marching into the third-floor penthouse office of Bob "Gucci-Only" Flint with his prisoner in tow. Or rather he didn't have him in toe as Waldemar O'Reilly was wearing smelly sneakers and the paranormal investigator did not want to dirty his hands on them. Instead his taloned fingers clutched O'Reilly by the collar and deposited him at the foot of Gucci-Only's desk.

"Here's your man," Tercero Mundo announced in his deep sepulchral baritone voice. "It was quite a chase but I promised I'd get him."

The Milwaukeean magazine magnate looked down from his desk chair with approval.

"His name is Waldemar O'Reilly," Tercero Mundo went on, "and I found him—"

"Yes, yes," Gucci-Only cut him off impatiently. "I know all about him."

"You do?"

"At the last minute I received outside help."

Gucci-Only indicated the far corner of the spacious office where sat the one and only Bart Starr, drink in hand and a naked woman on each arm.

"Naturally I offered him the amenities of the house," Gucci-Only added.

"Naturally," Tercero Mundo acceded.

"Still I'm glad you saved me the trouble of rounding him up."

"Which is well and good but what's Starr got to do with this?"

"I should let him explain."

Gucci-Only clapped his hands and the naked women at Starr's side absented themselves from the room, taking Starr's drink with them. The quarterback did not look happily on this.

"You can have them back once we're done," Gucci-Only promised.

"Very well," Starr said. "Here's the deal. As you may know, I have a cousin in England who's a drummer with a rock-and-roll band. They've toured America a couple of times and things happen where people come up to them with all sorts of wild schemes. So one day Richard—that's my cousin's name—let drop about this guy who approached him with a plot to seize control of the country. My cousin at first dismissed him as a kook—until he learned the guy's name." Starr paused for effect. "It was none other than Johnny Unitas."

"What?" Tercero Mundo's jaw dropped.

"I kid you not," Starr held up his hand in a Boy Scout oath. "America is a football nation. And the loss of a single team franchise would cause a domino effect that would wreck the entire structure, plunging the nation into financial ruin. He decided Green Bay was the most vulnerable target since its entire economy is dependent on that autographed football. With the Packers gone, the other teams will soon follow, after which Johnny would step in and declare himself ruler of the new Unitas States of America."

"But..." Tercero Mundo objected, "that doesn't make sense."

"Unitas admits there are still a few kinks that need working out. But the theory is sound. And in exchange for my cousin's support, Johnny offered to give him Texas, rechristening it the Lone Starr State."

"Then it was Unitas' idea to steal the football."

"Yes, only I beat him to it. It was I who hired Waldemar O'Reilly to make off with it. And it was I who let him hide out in my basement."

"Which could use heating," Waldemar O'Reilly interjected.

"Shut up. You're a cheap crook and if Unitas had hired you he'd've done the same thing. Anyhow my plan was to go to Unitas and secretly film him making a deal to buy the football from me, perhaps even offer to split Texas and call it Lone Starr One and Lone Starr Two. After which I'd expose him."

"Leading to the Colts firing him and in that way removing your biggest rival."

Starr shrugged. "There was that too," he admitted.

Tercero Mundo suspected there was more to it than what Starr had told them. He asked, point blank:

"What made you come here instead?"

"Well," Starr blushed slightly, "I have a friend here—I won't say who—"

"He means my secretary, Bambi," Gucci-Only provided.

"All right, Bambi. You know how it is with jocks on the road. One night Bambi let slip about Mr Flint's plans to turn Waldemar O'Reilly into an adult video phenomenon, so I thought..."

"He decided he wanted in on the deal," Gucci-Only finished the sentence for him.

"Only half of O'Reilly's cut," Starr pointed out. "It's not like I'm greedy."

Chapter 305

Lombardi did a double take when he saw Yumiko Raskolnikov had changed into long gown with a high slit up the side. Out of her leotards and in the dress the girl didn't look near as bony as she had at the museum. Instead she reminded Lombardi of a normal woman reduced to HO scale.

Had it been another time or place, and had he not been a devoted husband and father, this might have had an impact on him. But as it was his mind was on other things. Although he had to admit her skirt was alarmingly distracting, especially in the frigid Wisconsin night air.

"Is this the place?" Yumiko Raskolnikov asked, drawing her van to a halt before a modest mansion by the shores of Lake Superior, near where the solar turbine generators were located. "Ach du meine Güte! I recognize this place. It's the summer home of Johnny Unitas, the greatest quarterback of all time!"

"Oh, right," Lombardi grumbled. "As long as he isn't throwing interceptions."

"You say there'll be a reward for my helping you?"

"Well, yeah. Starr and Unitas put up $2000, remember? Not to mention the gallon of hot water I'm throwing in. Of course, I fully expect to get my cut of the $2000."

"Glcvpny znyr."

"What's that?"

"Lbh'er n terrql znyr onfgneq glvat gb purng zr bhg bs zl snve funer!"

"Good grief, sister, it was bad enough when you spoke languages I did know, but this is gibberish."

"Gibberish, is it?" Yumiko Raskolnikov seemed to change. And Lombardi didn't like it. "Ahornah lloigazath ot throdog Cthulhu ymg' mgvulgtlagln orr'enah ahna ng ymg' ah'r'luh ph'nglui shog ot syha'h li!"

He had no idea what she was saying. He only knew he didn't like it, and yanking open the door of Yumiko's van he tumbled onto the street where he hurriedly backed away.

Yumiko too jumped out of the van and advanced on him, her eyes glowing like white-hot coals as she reached down into a holster strapped to her thigh and pulled out a large pistol. Only instead of firing, she continued to voice her strange language:

"Ahornah ymg' ai soth mgng 'gibberish' rest ot ymg' yah'or'nanahh!"

"All right, that enough of that!" a voice rang out, and the next instant a bright spotlight shone down on the scene revealing Inspector Tonraq along with his officers and camera crew lying in wait. Mayor Adlartok was also present, standing in the background.

"Stop right there!" Yumiko spun about, facing them while pointing the gun menacingly in their direction. "Take one step and I'll—" At which point she caught sight of herself in the police car's side mirror. "Hold it a minute," she paused. "Let me just adjust this..." And she fixed her skirt to show more thigh. "There. That's better. You guys are filming this, right?"

"Don't try to sexy your way out of this, Miss Raskolnikov," Tonraq warned. "Or should I say Medusa Coil?"

The revelation struck the girl like a bolt of lightning; but only temporarily as she swiftly recovered.

"So you know my secret."

"Yes," Tonraq nodded solemnly. "I know you are, in the words of HP Lovecraft, *a negress*!"

"A what?" asked Mayor Adlartok, taken aback.

"A negress," Tonraq repeated. He then, seeing the confused look on the Mayor's face, added, "A black woman."

Adlartok sighed. It was a rather irritated sigh.

"In case it escaped your attention, Tonraq, so am I."

"You're a negress?"

"No, I'm black."

"Oh, right. I knew that."

"Then what's the big deal about Miss Raskolnikov, or Miss Coil if you will, being of black heritage?"

"Oh, well, sir, it has nothing to do with that. Perhaps Coach Lombardi should explain. After all, he's the one who put us wise to her. Right, Coach?"

Coach Lombardi, still on his hands and knees on the pavement, looked up and said, "Drizzle, drazzle, drizzle, drome; three quarks for Muster Mark's new home."

"Eh? Coach, I asked you to tell your end of the story."

"Bababadalgharaghtakamminarronnkonnbro
nntonnerronntuonnthunntrovarrhounawnskaw
ntoohoohoordenenthurnuk!" the coach
rejoiced.

"Coach!"

"You needn't bother," Yumiko-Medusa
laughed. "You'll never get anything out of him
again. He called my language gibberish; so I put
a curse on him that he should speak gibberish
as well. Although technically, that was a quote
from *Finnegan's Wake*. Still it's about as close
to gibberish as you can get."

"A curse?" Mayor Adlartok looked on in
amazement. "What kind of woman is this?"

"It's what I've been trying to tell you,"
Tonraq explained. "The woman's an Obeah
priestess from New Orleans!"

Chapter 306

"A *what* priestess?" the mayor looked about
in total confusion.

"It's a type of voodoo or hoodoo practice," Tonraq explained. "It's like this. It isn't widely known but Coach Lombardi is a big fan of rhythm and blues music and his all-time favorite act is the Ike and Tina Turner Review. When he saw Miss Raskolnikov's picture in the newspaper he immediately recognized her as a former Ikette named Medusa Coil."

"The Ikettes were the Turner's backup singers," Adlartok provided.

"Right. So the coach wondered why anyone would give up a well-paying job as an Ikette to become a starving artist."

"Makes sense. Then what?"

"Lombardi approached me with his suspicions so we cooked up this charade to throw suspicion on him to force Yumiko-Medusa into the open. My next step was to contact New Orleans police. They sent a man down to— But here. I'll let Björn take over."

"Björn?" the Mayor blinked.

"Yes, sir. You see, he's really Catfish Redbone, special agent for the New Orleans CID."

The man who had been Björn Yisterdae wiped the pasty make-up from his face, heaving a sigh of relief as he exclaimed: "Woooo-wee! Pwaise de lord an' halleluiah ah kins drop dis jive honkey ax-cent an' goes back ta talkin' normal; no-wam-sane? Yo still be filmin' dis, right?"

"On second thought," Mayor Adlartok suggested, "perhaps it'd be beter if Inspector Tonraq did the explaining."

"Coach Lombardi wondered if she might have something to do with the theft of the football, only we had nothing to tie her in with it. Catfish here informed us she'd been involved in some shady practices down in the Big Easy, things involving voodoo kangaroo stuff."

"I believe the word is 'congeroo'," a voice from out of nowhere spoke up.

All turned at the sound to see Tercero Mundo, tall, gaunt, in Inverness coat and slouch hat, standing behind them, both feet several inches above the ground.

"Gorblimey and cat's whiskers!" Mayor Adlartok exclaimed. "What sorcery is this?"

"No sorcery at all," Tercero Mundo assured them. "I am merely sensitive to all things paranormal, so when I detected the presence of a conjure woman in the vicinity of Johnny Unitas' summer house—"

A sudden scream interrupted him, splitting the night as Yumiko-Medusa took off in a mad dash for freedom. Tercero Mundo saw only one thing to do and he did it. He leaped forward and landed on the back of the figure, bearing her to the ground. An instant later his talon-like grip closed on the revolver and he wrested it away.

"As I was saying—" Tercero Mundo resumed, only to be interrupted again by...

"Hey!"

...the sudden appearance of Johnny Unitas running out of his house.

"What all this noise out here?"

"Officer, arrest that man!" Tercero Mundo pointed. "He's been plotting the overthrow of the United States!"

"Are you crazy?" Unitas shouted back. "I'm the guy who's been trying to prevent it!"

Chapter 307

The situation which had started out as merely confusing had degenerated into something totally incomprehensible. Here was the person Green Bay's own Bart Starr claimed had approached his cousin Richard with a plan to overthrow the United States and set up his own empire. An enormous gust of frigid Arctic air blew in from Lake Superior turning all who'd gathered outside the Unitas home into human popsicles, while the conjure woman in her flimsy dress became a solitary goose pimple.

"Now just a minute," Mayor Adlartok attempted to make sense of it all. "You... What's your name?"

"Tercero Mundo."

"You, Tercero Mundo, are telling me the great Johnny Unitas is turning his back on his own country and plotting its overthrow? Honestly, sir, I'll concede he's a hated rival and the citizens of Green Bay regard him as a rotten fink, but even so I find it impossible to believe him capable of treason."

"Nevertheless," Tercero Mundo insisted, "I have it on good authority—"

"Oh, for heaven's sake." Unitas threw his hands in the air. "Geewillikers with a cherry on top. Don't tell me Bart Starr told you that idiotic story about my talking to his cousin. Odds bodkins, can't you guys take a joke? If I wanted to overthrow the government do you think I'd let that blabbermouth get wind of it?"

"Then you mean he hired Waldemar O'Reilly to steal the autographed football for nothing?" Tercero Mundo asked.

"Ah, so he *did* do it," Unitas smacked his palm. "I knew he was connected somehow. Why, that man's as much a tightwad as Lombardi, perhaps bigger, so I knew something had to be up when he joined me in offering a reward."

"You mean he knew it'd never be collected."

"Exactly. You know, not all jocks are dumb. Some of us are capable of grasping more than five football plays." He glanced down at Lombardi. "I mean, really. Run to the left, run to the right, run up the middle, downfield pass, and kick. You could write his entire playbook on the back of a cocktail napkin."

"You must admit it saves money on printing costs," Inspector Tonraq came to the coach's defense.

"Yes," Mayor Adlartok added. "And look at all those southern colleges who eliminated the pass altogether. At least our players *can* memorize five plays."

"I think we're getting off subject," Tercero Mundo broke in. "If this entire theft is based on a misunderstanding then why do I still feel a sense of looming danger for both the city and the nation?"

"Heck if I know," Unitas shrugged. "You're the psycho, not me."

"It's not psycho, it's psychic," Tercero Mundo corrected him. "And I only said I'm sensitive to paranormal activity."

"Well I'll tell you what it is," the human goose pimple conjure woman cackled. "It's the end of the world as we know it!"

"Are you quoting another yet-to-be-recorded song?"

"I'm telling you that when Gucci-Only films his porno movie tonight—"

"What porno movie?" Tonraq asked.

"Tell you later," Tercero Mundo answered.

"I'm telling you when Gucci-Only makes his movie, he'll unknowing unleash the forces of Hell upon the world. Great Cthulhu will rise from his prison—"

"Great who?" Tonraq asked again.

"HP Lovecraft," Tonraq answered again. "Tell you—"

"I know. You'll tell me later."

"But wait!" Tercero Mundo turned to address the conjure woman. "If you know about the porno movie it could only mean—"

"It means I engineered the whole thing, playing all of you for fools. While y'all concerned yourselves over the theft of a stupid football—"

"I wouldn't necessarily call it 'stupid'," Adlartok threw in defensively.

"—I laid the foundation for Great Cthulhu's return to dominate the Earth!"

"Great gloriosky!" Tercero Mundo regarded the woman scornfully. "You fink! You rotten fink!"

"Rottener than Starr?" asked Mayor Adlartok.

"A thousand times more," declared Tercero Mundo who then turned and took Inspector Tonraq by his coat lapels. "Quick, man! There's no time to lose! We must go there and stop that filming at once!"

"Especially if they don't have a permit," Tonraq agreed, hurrying his people into their squad cars.

"Sir?" one of the officers stopped him. "What about the Coach?"

They regarded Lombardi, who regarded them back.

"In the name of Annah the Allmaziful," he babbled rejoicefully, "the Everliving, the Bringer of Plurabilities, haloed be her eve, her singtime sung, her rill be run, unhemmed as it is uneven!"

Tonraq rubbed his chin, giving it some thought.

"Actually," he observed thoughtfully, "the man never was that articulate a speaker. I say we turn him over to the Packers organization and as long as we don't say anything no will ever be the wiser."

Chapter 308

Time passed, which proved beneficial for everyone's existence. Whether time would continue to pass was a matter of conjecture.

On the long drive over, Tercero Mundo told Inspector Tonraq all he knew about HP Lovecraft, Cthulhu, Gucci-Only, Waldemar O'Reilly, the porno film, and everything else that had occurred along the way. Tonraq in turn filled Tercero Mundo in on all that had taken place on his end.

"That's why I carry this cushion," he concluded. "The sores are terrible!"

Unitas gave a fuller explanation of his involvement as well, so by the time they arrived outside Gucci-Only's penthouse office everyone had achieved a mutual state of understanding—or confusion, as the case may be. Fortunately everything was being captured on film so they could review it at a later date if need be.

"Odd's bodkins," Mayor Adlartok shook his head, trying to clear room for these new developments. "I must say this has certainly been an interesting case. Let's pray we are in time to recover the football and prevent the end of the world."

It was good to know, as a city official, he had his priorities in order.

"Recover your silly football if you can," the conjure woman taunted them. "But it will not prevent the return of the Old One! Iä! Iä! Cthulhu fhtagn! Iä! Iä! Y'kaa haa hoii. Wza-y'ei! Great is Cthulhu!"

Again Adlartok shook his head. "There she goes spouting gib—"

Tercero Mundo clamped a hand over the Mayor's mouth before he could complete the word.

"Careful, sir," he warned. "Remember what she did to Coach Lombardi. The last thing we'd want is for a political figure to talk nonsense."

* * *

Filming was just getting underway in Gucci-Only's studio on Waldemar O'Reilly's debut film, *The Pickle Man Cometh*, when Tercero Mundo and the others arrived. Gucci-Only, Starr, and the rest of the crew startled as the unexpected crowd burst in. A lush scene had been laid out with candles and incense. Waldemar O'Reilly lay naked with a trio of beauties at his side. Behind them, serving as a backdrop, was Yumiko-Medusa's reproduction of *Nude With Pickle*, the one that had led to Gucci-Only's discovery of his new film star. An unfathomable smile crossed the painter's face as she gazed upon her work.

"It will not be long," she commented enigmatically. "It will not be long."

"Well let's hope it is," Gucci-Only retorted. "Otherwise nobody's going to watch the movie."

"Mr Flint," Tonraq approached him. "I order you to cease filming at once."

"What do you mean?" Gucci-Only demanded. "You've no jurisdiction here."

"You'd best do what he says," Tercero Mundo suggested. "You don't realize what dark forces are at work."

"Dark forces?" Gucci-Only blinked. "Oh, you mean the girls. It's true two of them are non-Caucasian but you shouldn't concern yourself over that. It's a new era of equality, you know, and to that end we lined up three women to appear with Waldemar O'Reilly in this scene, one white, one black, and one brown. The brown one, Moana Lot, is from Hawaii. You'll note she has a nice tan."

"Yes," Tercero Mundo agreed. "All over."

Gucci-Only went on: "The black chick is Selma Azz from Alabama, and the white one is—"

"Miss Bambi!" Tercero Mundo recognized her. "You do this on the side?"

"On the side, on the back, from the rear, whatever," Miss Bambi shrugged. "Anything so long as it pays."

At that moment one of the film crew—not the one following Inspector Tonraq, but the guys filming the movie—interrupted things, saying: "Hey, something's wrong with the painting!"

Yumiko-Medusa laughed as the others turned to face it. The paint, it turned out, was running down the mirrored glass surface on which she had painted it.

"The heat from the lights is melting it," Tercero Mundo cried out.

"Aw, who cares," Gucci-Only dismissed it. "It was only a prop."

"Fools!" Yumiko-Medusa cackled with insane laughter. "Iä! Iä! A prop you say. Fools again! Know you not that yon mirrored surface serves as a portal to the other side—a doorway through which Great Cthulhu may enter this world?"

Chapter 309

"Odds bodkins!' Mayor Adlartok was moved to say. "I thought y'all said Cthulhu was already on this Earth, sleeping in his sunken underwater city of R'yleh."

"Don't look at me," Inspector Tonraq held up his hands. "It was the psycho who said it."

"For the last time," Tercero Mundo corrected them, "I'm a Paranormal Private Investigator. I have no powers or control over psychic—or psycho—phenomena."

"Oh yeah?" Adlartok regarded him with disapproval. "Then why is it your feet don't touch the ground?"

"Guys, please!" Starr and Unitas joined as one to break up the fight. "There's a big ugly thing with the face of an octopus looking down at us from the other side of the glass. And he doesn't look all that friendly."

"Iä! Iä!" Yumiko-Medusa again cackled. "Cthulhu fhtagn! Iä! Iä! Y'kaa haa hoii. Wza-y'ei! Great is Cthulhu!"

"Could somebody please get her to shut up?" Tonraq asked. "Put a gag on her or something."

A moment later it was done and Tercero Mundo accessed the situation.

"We must stop Great Cthulhu before he crosses the portal," he announced. "There's no other way. Somebody has to enter his world and face him."

Nobody took a step forward to volunteer.

"I said," Tercero Mundo repeated, "somebody has to enter Cthulhu's world and face him."

"Gee, I'd love to help," Unitas spoke up, "only I'm scheduled to appear at a Kiwanis Club breakfast tomorrow."

"Me too," Starr echoed. "And after that I promised Coach Lombardi I'd try to design a sixth play we could try sometime. I was thinking either an end-around or Statue of Liberty. "

"I've got an awful lot of paperwork piled on my desk," Gucci-Only tossed in.

"And we have all this film to develop," both camera crews demurred.

"Great," Tercero Mundo sighed and took the Inspector by the hand. "Come along, Tonraq. It's up to you and me to cross over."

"Now just a minute, Mundo," Tonraq shook himself loose. "I take exception to your terminology. I happen to be a happily married man and I don't go for that sort of thing. Just because you're a little light in the loafers—" He glanced down at Tercero Mundo's feet, their customary two inches above the ground, and the implication was obvious.

"Oh, don't be ridiculous," Tercero Mundo rebuked him angrily. He then lifted one foot. "If you look closely you'll see my soles are made of clear plastic so it only appears I'm hovering in air. It's an illusion to throw others off guard."

"Well," Tonraq marveled. "It certainly fooled me. Still, if you think I'm going in there to face that monstrous giant—"

"It's another illusion, Tonraq; a magnification. From our point of view, Cthulhu appears to be enormous. But once inside you'll find he's no bigger than the rest of us."

Still Tonraq hesitated. "I don't know. He looks awful large to me."

"Very well," Tercero Mundo said at length. "Then perhaps Mayor Adlartok would accompany me instead."

"Gosh, Mundo, you know I'd really love to," the Mayor backed away, "only this looks like it could take some time and I have to be up early tomorrow. I'm delivering the keynote address at that same Kiwanis Club breakfast.."

One did not have to be feasting at Belshazzar's table to see the writing on the wall. Nobody wanted to accompany Tercero Mundo into that frightful realm so he would have to go it alone.

Wasting little time on useless admonitions, the paranormal investigator stepped across.

It was a strange land he entered, filled with swirling mists and strange shifting lights. Mysterious aromas assailed his nostrils, some not all together unpleasant. A short way in, Great Cthulhu sat at a modest table, a water pitcher at his side. An extra chair had been provided for Tercero Mundo to sit. The Great Old One remained impassive as Tercero Mundo seated himself across from him. Only the octopus-like tendrils of his face moved as both sized the other up. Cthulhu greeted Tercero Mundo with a series of rhythmic finger snaps that ended with four melodic fillips on his neck. Tercero Mundo responded in kind and the conversation got underway.

Chapter 310

Mundo: Thoo-loo!

Cthulhu: Yoo-hoo!

Mundo: You like to speak Canarsie?

Cthulhu: I like to talk Canarsie!

Mundo: Rasbanyas yata bene fuchi atimeni kharonchi, that, how do you say, that flatfoot, he asky-tasky what you wan, you gaddit?

Cthulhu: Nya tink!

Mundo: Nya tink?

Cthulhu: Only takee-over orld-way.

Mundo: Oh, boy! (Gets up and walks to the portal window, speaks to Tonraq:) The Great Thoo-loo—

Cthulhu: Yoo-hoo! Rasbanyas yata bene fuchi atimeni—

Mundo: Quiet! I'm negotiating!

Cthulhu: Oh! (He peers out through the portal and points:) Caterer?

Mundo (nods:) Caterer.

Cthulhu: Rasbanyas yata bene fuchi atimeni kharonchi, likah yum-yum tasty tart.

Tonraq: What'd he say?

Mundo: He said he'd like a tart.

(The three girls shrug and head toward the portal opening.)

Mundo: He means a pastry.

Girls: Oh, gotcha.

Mundo (calling to caterer:) What kind of goodies have you got?

Caterer: I got vanilla cream and raspberry. You want I should give him the raspberry?

Mundo: No, I don't think that'd be wise. But let me check. (Returns to Cthulhu and again sits opposite him.) Thoo-loo!

Cthulhu: Yoo-hoo!

Mundo (gives him a three-finger wave:) Ello doh!

Cthulhu (returns the gesture:) Ello dah!

Mundo: Rasbanyas yata bene fuchi atimeni kharonchi, that, how do you call it, that Barney Boy, he asky-tasky what flavorski you fertsaig, ingensommen?

Cthulhu: Rasbanyas yata bene fuchi atimeni kharonchi, pareditima hiha. Fergidda pastry. Wanna football.

Mundo: Sure dat?

Cthulhu: Sure dat.

(Mundo returns to portal opening.)

Mundo: He wants the football. It was promised to him as an offering.

Adlartok: Ask Great Thoo-loo—

Cthulhu: (Rising, facing the wrong direction) Yoo-hoo! Rasbanyas yata bene fuchi atimeni kharonchi—

Mundo (to Mayor:) Sorry, the visibility's not good in here. (To Cthulhu:) Sit down, you Squamous Squidhead!

Cthulhu: Oh, shut up, I don't have to! (Goes into a silent snit.) Rasbanyas yata bene fuchi, fergidda football. Y' gotha zvag pbaqvgvba nhgbtencurq Joe Namath ebbxvr pneq!

Mundo (swallows hard:) Oh boy. (Smiles uncomfortably:) We shall see; we shall see. (Rises and exits portal window.)

Chapter 311

"Well?" Adlartok and Tonraq demanded.

"It's worse than I thought," Tercero Mundo shuddered. "Great Cthulhu—"

"Yoo-hoo!" the Ancient One called out.

"Would you be quiet? I'm working on it!" He gave his attention back to the Mayor and Inspector. In a low voice he whispered, "Great Cthulhu wants nothing less than a mint-condition, autographed Joe Namath rookie card!"

"Oh my God!" Adlartok clutched his chest and would have fainted had not Tonraq been there to catch him. "How— How—" He couldn't finish.

"Heaven's sake, Mundo," Tonraq nearly shouted. "Does he know what he's asking? We could search the whole state and never turn up a Joe Namath card. No one here would dream of having one!"

"I'm fully aware of that," Tercero Mundo persisted. "Still we have to do something or Green Bay, the State of Wisconsin, perhaps the entire planet will be doomed."

Starr and Unitas stepped up.

"When you say, 'the entire planet', does that include Baltimore?" Unitas asked.

"Yes," Tercero Mundo replied. "I'm afraid it does."

Unitas turned to face Starr.

"Look here, Bert—"

"It's Bart."

"Whatever. We can't let this otherworldly thing get away with this. Destroying the planet is one thing, but to threaten a football city goes beyond the pale."

"I assume that includes saving Green Bay as well?" Starr put in.

"Yeah, well, if we gotta." Unitas looked around. "Somebody toss me the football." The ball was still sitting where Waldemar O'Reilly had been filming his scene. Gucci-Only went to fetch it but Unitas told him: "Be sure to wipe it off first."

Gucci-Only tossed the ball to Unitas but Starr stepped in front of him and caught it first. "Yo, Cthulhu!" he called out.

"Yoo-hoo!" the Great Old One responded. "Rasbanyas yata bene fuchi—"

"Oh knock it off! We can't give you a Joe Namath card. It's out of the question. It's the football or nothing."

Tonraq, Adlartok, Unitas, and the others rushed to his side screaming, "No! You can't!"

But Starr relied on his expert scrambling skills to elude them.

"Go long!" he called, and Great Cthulhu did as he was told, retreating into his dark realm. Starr fired a perfect spiral directly at the mirror...

Only it wasn't all that direct after all. The ball sailed upward and instead of entering the mirrored portal, struck the frame above it.

A great crackling sound followed as the glass entryway cracked and shattered. Yumiko-Medusa broke away from the officers holding her and raced for the dwindling opening, shouting "No!" For reasons known only to herself she dragged the naked Waldemar O'Reilly along with her.

Yumiko-Medusa entered the dark world of the Ancient Ones just as the doorway closed upon itself, never to be seen again.

Waldemar O'Reilly was not so fortunate. He was but partially inside when it sealed itself off from the world. The would-be film star lost a bit of chest hair... and a few other things that preceded him. One of them stayed inside Cthulhu's world; the other two hit the floor as Waldemar O'Reilly clutched his lower abdomen, howling in pain at his loss.

The film director, upon seeing this too-graphic display, yelled, "Cut!"

To which Waldemar O'Reilly replied, "Yes, badly."

The man did eventually recover, but he would never make another adult video. He no longer had what it takes to qualify for the role, although he later found a place in the soprano section of the church choir.

With order restored, and the world, including Baltimore, saved from destruction, Unitas glared at Starr, angered over his usurping the position he had meant to play.

"Aw man," he pouted, "that's what I was gonna do."

Starr merely smiled and patted the unfortunate quarterback on the head. "Only with your luck, you'd have been intercepted."

"I think you are both to be congratulated," Tercero Mundo praised them. "You acted well in recognizing a conspiracy and doing your best to prevent it."

The word struck home and they shook hands in the spirit of sportsmanship.

Tercero Mundo retrieved the autographed football from the pile of broken glass and handed it to Mayor Adlartok. "I believe this is yours; or rather, the city's." He took a moment to reflect on all that had happened. Heroes had stepped to the fore, good men had done their jobs, yet not without losses. Gucci-Only did not get the movie he wanted, and poor Waldemar O'Reilly, a senseless pawn in the mad scheme, would never produce another drop of testerone. But as with everything, there are winners and losers. It is the luck of the draw, or as Tercero Mundo aptly concluded, "That's just the way the balls bounce."

Chapter 312

An end comes to all things. Although no one can say ends are ever permanent. Tercero Mundo sat alone in the movie studio, Adlartok, Tonraq, Gucci-Only, Starr, Unitas, Catfish Redbone, the three women, the cameramen, the caterer, and all the rest having left to tell their friends a story that would never be believed. Nor was there any proof to support their claims. Cthulhu's body had given off a level of radiation which fogged the camera film, rendering it useless. Perhaps this was for the best.

With the sacred autographed football once more in its possession, Green Bay would grow and prosper, Lombardi, even in his diminished capacity, would continue to coach, and Starr and Unitas continue their on-field rivalry.

What lay ahead Tercero Mundo could only imagine. Certainly he was not fool enough to believe Great Cthulhu had been defeated. If one pathway existed allowing access from his world to this, then surely others could be found as well. And the Ancient One would surely hold Tercero Mundo responsible, for he had negotiated in good faith only to be tricked by a clever ruse. Otherworldly beings do not appreciate being made fools of. Their patience is great, and they have all the time in the world to exact it.

These thoughts and more ran through Tercero Mundo's mind. A shuffling of feet interrupted him and he looked up to find a handsome, athletic young man standing before him.

"Hello," the young man greeted him. "My name's Joe Namath and I happened to be in town when I heard someone was asking for my autograph. I brought my pen with me so if you could point him out..."

* * *

Afterward to *Nude With Pickle*
and Introduction to the Short Stories

This concludes my reconstruction of *Nude With Pickle*, presented in an edited and condensed format due to the damaged condition of the materials available.

Nothing is ever truly lost, and somewhere in the hands of an antiquarian collector, an out-of-the-way bookshop, a dusty library, or lining a kitchen shelf exist more samples of Hoo's literary output. Perhaps someday those missing samples will find their way into our hands. Fortunately in my efforts to uncover *Nude With Pickle* I came upon several unrelated short stories by the author, five of which I present here to give the reader a sampling of his wide range of interests.

Even now sufficient material is at hand for another collection of stories should the public demand. And there is always the possibility that missing installments of *Nude With Pickle* may turn up.

Until then, I hope you enjoyed this brief and rare glimpse into the mind of a one-of-a-kind author and pray it will inspire others to seek out other lesser known writers deserving of recognition.

* * *

Are You Lonesome Tonight

(From the *Guava Grapevine*, April 4, 1960)

"Is your heart filled with pain?"

The music plays low and the background singers soft. A single muted spotlight shines down as the King launches into his monologue:

"I wonder, do you miss me?

"My life was empty before we met. I went to a matchmaking service, told them I wanted someone small and well-dressed who liked to swim. For six months I dated a penguin.

"Then you came along. I don't know what it was that threw us together. Whether it was fate, or chance, or just the fact we had the same parole officer.

"The times we had. I still remember that day you drove your car into the wall of a theater. You said it was just a stage you were going thru.

"Then you changed; it made no cents and you gave no quarter.

"A wise man said: Once a king always a king, but once a night is enough. I never knew what he meant by that.

"All I know is you came into my life like a whirlwind. You turned my world upside down, and I don't know how I'm going to get that stuff off the ceiling."

The Scream of the Butterfly

(From the *Guava Grapevine*, August 21, 1966)

"Your only friend until the end"

"You must forgive me," he apologized. "Since losing my Korean housekeeper I've been quite disoriented."

"I understand," Karen commiserated. "Shall I wear the French maid uniform?"

Hindley looked her over. She was young, slim, and graceful. "I'd like nothing better."

"Okay," she gave in. "But it'll cost you extra."

* * *

Karen woke to a noise at her door. Pale moonlight cast grotesque shadows across the floor.

"Who is it?" she called out, rising from bed to find her robe missing. She crossed the room to her closet and found it empty as well.

"It is I," a voice answered. "The ghost of Heathcliff."

"If you're a ghost," she asked it, "why don't you walk through the door?"

"Who said I was dead?" the voice countered, and Karen fainted.

* * *

"Are you all right?" Hindley knelt over her, rubbing her hand. "I heard you scream."

"I don't recall screaming," Karen responded.

"All the same I heard one."

* * *

It was several days later that she broached the subject. Holding her dusting fan at a discrete angle, she entered Hindley's reading room and asked, "Who was Heathcliff?"

"My brother," he answered, adjusting his moth-eaten smoking jacket. "We never got along. He fancied himself a scientist; always studying bugs. Had some silly belief about transmigration of souls. Nonsense really. Found him dead in his laboratory, hunched over a cage of butterflies. Buried him, released them, and that was that."

"You're sure they were butterflies?"

"Fairly sure; might've been moths. Who cares?"

Yes, thought Karen; it would account for the disappearance of my wardrobe.

* * *

Karen's employment ended shortly thereafter. When Hindley failed to appear for breakfast she found him dead beneath a blanket of Lepidoptera. Thankfully the French maid outfit was stored in mothballs so she had something to wear when leaving the house. She closed the door to echoing laughter that cried out, "Who said I was dead?"

It's a Family Affair

(From the *Guava Grapevine*, September 6, 1971)

"You see, it's in the blood"

What's in a name? Who can say? In earlier times, a man was called after his profession: Taylor, Singer, Smith, Mason, Miller, and so on. My family name was Ennay. My parents christened me Dexter. Somewhere in high school a wiseacre shortened it to "Dee". Dee Ennay, get it? Did that have anything to do with me studying chemistry and biology at college? Or would I have followed the same path had I been christened Mortimer Snerd? It's a moot point now, for I never made a name in science. Fame and recognition eluded me, and I ended up running a pharmacy with a small laboratory in the back.

"I know about your background," Mr Montague said from behind the fancy mahogany desk in his plush office. "I did my homework, which is something my son ought to have been doing instead of getting into trouble."

I looked around. To one side of the desk sat a big lunk of a fellow, young, college-aged, with arrogance written all over his face.

"Aw, c'mon, Dad," he scowled. "Your lawyers can get me out of it. It wouldn't be the first time."

"That's the problem, Romeo," Mr Montague replied, with a rising note in his voice. "It *isn't* the first time. Or the second, or the third, or even—"

"All right, all right; skip it."

I was coming to like the big lunk less and less each time he opened his mouth.

"What is it you wish me to do?" I asked.

Mr Montague leaned forward on his desk, with folded hands moving piston-like back and forth before his chin.

"Back in your professorial days, you gave a presentation—"

"Which got me kicked out of academia," I interrupted, sensing where this was going. It was the reason I was now a pharmacist and not head of a research firm.

"You gave a presentation," Mr Montague went on, unperturbed, "where you claimed human DNA could be altered by artificial means. You stated—"

"I stated that catalytic agents could be introduced into a living system and, over time, alter the structure of basic amino acids resulting in changes to that person's overall makeup. I meant it as a way of curing inherited diseases and weakened immune systems. The newspapers misreported it, saying I wanted to build a race of supermen, and I was let go from the university."

"Yes, yes," Montague waived it aside. "You needn't explain. I wouldn't understand the process and Romeo could care less, much as is his attitude about everything."

The lunk sank lower in his chair but said nothing.

"I ask again, what is it you want me to do?"

Montague glanced over at his son, then at me.

"Romeo has gotten himself in trouble... again. For some reason he believes my money along with his ability to toss a football gives him free access to any female he chooses."

"I see." I finally recognized the name, Romeo Montague. "You're the guy who raped two freshmen co-eds and a cheerleader."

"Allegedly raped," Montague put in.

"Did he?" I asked, looking in the boy's direction.

His reply was a contemptuous snort, as if to say, "So what if I did?"

My dislike for the arrogant bastard turned to outright contempt.

"I ask for the third time, what do you want me to do?"

Montague came to the point.

"Romeo left semen and saliva samples everywhere. DNA tests confirm it's his. I want you to change that."

"You want I should break into the police lab and—"

"Don't be an idiot. My lawyers can file motions to keep his case from going to trial for a year; maybe more. That gives you time to develop your DNA altering process and use it on Romeo; after which we'll introduce our own samples which will clear him."

If it were up to me I'd've thrown his sorry ass in prison where he'd gain a whole new respect for the idea of rape. But then, I was poor. And I'd been laughed at. Mr Montague must have sensed what I was thinking.

"You realize this can never get out. Fame will continue to elude you. But I will reward you handsomely. And I know people in similar situations who would avail themselves of your process—provided it works."

"Oh, it'll work," I assured him. "I've experimented successfully with lab animals and there's no reason it shouldn't work on humans as well." That's assuming Romeo Montague could be called human.

"Good." Montague handed me a check. "Then you're further along than I thought. Go back to your lab, close your pharmacy, and call me when you have something you know will do the job. And remember, you only have a year to do it."

"I'll have it for you in six weeks," I told him as I walked out the door.

* * *

Six weeks to the day, Montague and Romeo were in my lab. Romeo flinched at the sight of the hypodermic needle I held out before him.

"One shot of this and—"

"How does it work?" he asked, finally showing some interest. Like all bullies he was a coward at heart.

"It combines my catalytic agent with another form of DNA."

"Human DNA?" Mr Montague asked.

"No," I smiled. "That would be too risky. It would be absorbed by Romeo's preexisting DNA and the effect would be negligible. This uses animal DNA—"

"Like hell it does!" Romeo jumped from the table.

"Look, kid," I grew belligerent. "I can always reopen my pharmacy. What do you think you'll be opening once you're behind bars?"

"That's enough, Ennay," Montague interjected. "Go on with your explanation."

"I was going to say the animal DNA will intermingle with the human one, changing it enough so it no longer resembles the original. It's not like he'll grow rabbit ears or anything."

Somehow that appealed to Romeo's twisted sense of humor.

"You're all right, Doc." I wasn't a doctor. "Maybe you could throw in some horse genes to give me a bigger—"

"Be quiet, Romeo," Montague cut him off. "How long will it be before the changes take effect?"

"I'd give it a week; maybe two just to be certain."

"Fine," Montague nodded. "Let's do it."

* * *

I was living comfortably off Montague's checks when, several months later, there was a knock at my door. I bid the maid answer it and show whoever it was into the den.

She did, cringing as she conducted Mr Montague and a hairy hulking brute into the room. Despite the pulled down hat and turned up collar I recognized it as Romeo.

"You did this to me!" he cried, lurching forward. "You made me into this!"

I looked up into the simian features and calmly invited him to sit down.

"By the way, may I offer you a banana?"

"Cut the comedy, Ennay," Montague bellowed. "You never said anything about making my boy into a monkey."

"I believe he did a good enough job of that on his own. Our deal was to clear him of a rape charge, which I did. As for any side effects..."

"You said there'd be none."

"No," I shook my head. "All I said was he wouldn't grow rabbit ears."

"If you think you can get away with this—" Montague grew threatening but I cut him off.

"What will you do? Go to the DA and admit you tampered with evidence? Have the boy retried and sent to jail? Confess you've been paying me hush money ever since?"

"Okay, Ennay," Montague quietened, seeing it was no use. "I guess I had it coming. Come on, Romeo. Let's get out of here."

"But he promised me a banana," Romeo protested.

"I'll buy you one on the way home."

That was the last I saw of either of them. To my knowledge Romeo never got within ten feet of another woman, although in time his extended arms could have stretched that far. The monthly checks from Montague came less frequently and finally stopped. I didn't mind because I'd invested them wisely, most of it in Montague Industries stock. I wished him all the best.

Meanwhile I could relax with a clear conscience. Ethical questions regarding what I had done did not bother me. After all, the only thing I promised was that Romeo wouldn't grow rabbit ears. What I didn't say was that the cheerleader he raped was my sister's daughter. Merciful Fate threw him into my hands. And just as Montague had acted on behalf of his family, I had done the same for mine.

Sunset Grill

(From the *Guava Grapevine*, September 19, 1984)

"It's the kind that eats you up inside"

"Hello, Mom?" Barbara Quillem held the phone close, hoping it would improve the connection. "What? Oh, Australia's great; so beautiful; and such nice people. I met this wonderful guy. His name's Ryan and... No, Mother, I'm not fooling around. Yes, Mother, I'm being careful."

Barbara was glad her mother couldn't see the expression on her face. Or the one she'd had last night when Ryan drove her to ecstasy, telling her she was the best thing he'd ever tasted. He was the only guy she'd let get away with calling her "Barbie".

"Mom," she confided, "I think it's the real thing. He's asked me out to dinner and... Mom?

You're breaking up. Listen, I'll call back later. Okay. Bye."

* * *

"Smells good," Ethan complimented Ryan as he grabbed another snag. "That Shiela you brought is cracker."

"Isn't she?" Ryan agreed. "Vejjos are always best."

"Bit of a silly nong though. I mean, you did say you wanted her for dinner."

"Yeh," Ryan shrugged as he fired up the Barbie. "And I was honest when I told her she was the best thing I ever tasted."

And Justice For All

(From the *Guava Grapevine*, August 25, 1984)

"Rolls of red tape seal your lips"

The Medical Examiner was giving his testimony, "The victim was struck in the back of the head by a blunt instrument..." when an angry voice from the rear of the courtroom cut him off.

"That does it!" A prosperous looking gentleman jumped to his feet.

Murmurs filled the room as the judge called for order.

"What's the meaning of this?" His Honor demanded. "By what right do you interrupt these proceedings?"

"Every right in the world," the man at the back answered. "My name's Andrew Blunt, president and CEO of Blunt Instruments, Inc. For years now I've listened to you people besmirch my product. Now I've had enough and I demand you stop or I'll sue every one of you."

"Can he do that?" the judge asked the DA.

"Don't ask me," Mr Burger shrugged. "You're the one with the gavel."

The judge scratched his head. "What if we said the murderer used a solid object?"

"Aw, no you don't," another man rose from the gallery. "I'll not let you tarnish the name of Jack Solid."

The judge stared at the ceiling then down at the ME. "What exactly was the victim struck with?"

"A walking stick, Your Honor."

"Fine." The judge looked out from the bench. "Does anybody have a problem with that?"

A timid brown hand raised itself into the air and...

* * *

"You see," Judge Hardy told the bartender that evening, "his name was Joaquin and he carves these little sticks..." His words slurred as he polished off the fifth boilermaker.

"So you ended up tossing the case because of insufficient evidence?"

"Oh, there was Eva Dents — along with Whit Ness and Tess T Mony and..."

He set the empty mug on the counter and looked around the busy tavern.

"You know, Sam, days like this make me think I took the wrong bar exam."

Nude With Pickle

James Hold

Thank you for reading my book.
You can find more tales by this author by searching the
internet.

Remember downloads are free but reviews are priceless.
Please send comments or suggestions to
jamesroyhold@gmail.com

www.ingramcontent.com/pod-product-compliance
Lightning Source LLC
Chambersburg PA
CBHW071332140726
47996CB00005B/1942